This Mammoth belongs to

....

Caroline Binch on Tags,
her own dream horse

For
Mazza,
Ramona,
& the Ballymun jockeys

First published in Great Britain 1999
by Mammoth
an imprint of Egmont Children's Books Limited
239 Kensington High Street, London, W8 6SA
Text and illustrations copyright © Caroline Binch 1999
Caroline Binch has asserted her moral rights
A CIP catalogue record for this title
is available from the British Library
ISBN 0 7497 4294 1
Printed in Hong Kong
by Wing King Tong Ltd
10 9 8 7 6 5 4 3 2

Christy's Dream

Caroline Binch

Christy had wanted a pony for as long as he could remember.
"Oh, he's always been soft on the ponies," his ma would say.
His da didn't say much at all, only, "Ah, is that so, Christy?"

Christy knew everything about horses and ponies. He loved reading about them and knew that one day he would have one of his own. For years now, he had been saving most of his birthday and pocket money. He minded people's dogs and helped out at home. He would soon make his dream come true.

Christy had a big family. Their flat was always full of brothers and sisters, nephews and nieces. That didn't bother Christy. He had never known it any other way.

Christy wasn't at home much anyway. When not at school, he was at the stables looking after the horses with his friends. Horsey, who ran the horse project, taught the boys all about horses and how to look after them.

Some of the boys had their own horses. They kept them tethered to goalposts on the playing fields or to lamp posts on the grass verges around the estate. Christy was able to ride but only when his friends felt like it. Sometimes they rode double or raced each other. That was the best – galloping along at top speed.

Christy felt happiest with the horses. He loved the warm sweet smell of them. He liked listening to their teeth tearing at the grass and grinding it down.

Sometimes he ate grass himself, just to be like them. And he would blow air through his lips to horse-talk, the way they snorted out of their soft nostrils.

Christy's longing for his own horse would make his insides ache. He knew just what he wanted, a lively filly with a passion for speed.

Christy's grandad had promised to take him to the horse market at Smithfield. Granda lived close by and Christy loved to hear his stories about working with racehorses when he was young. "Oh, there's not a creature in all creation more lovely, more graceful," he would say softly.

"When I'm a jockey," said Christy, "I'm going to win all the Irish races, then beat the English at Newmarket."

Granda chuckled, "I've no doubt you will, Christy, you'll do us proud."

There was only one problem - Ma! She was dead against the horses.
"You're not having one," she'd say, "and you can forget about them jockey notions. Haven't I enough to do without horses and jockeys to worry about?"

Da loved the horses. "A jockey would be a fine job, Christy," he'd say. "You'd make your old da very happy."

It was a clear wintry day when Granda and Christy went to Smithfield.

"We'll just have a quick look and see what's on offer, young Christy," said Granda.

But Christy had bigger plans. Without telling anyone, he'd taken out all his savings. He wasn't leaving without a pony!

The market was busy and exciting. Christy felt very small in amongst the men and their horses. He stuck close to Granda. The air was thick with shouting and the clattering of hooves and the loud snorting and whinnying of the horses.

Christy fell in love at Smithfield. She was a beautiful grey filly, with dark, dark eyes and a silver tail.

"That's my horse, Granda," he cried. "She's the one I've been dreaming about." Christy could hardly bear it.

"Oh, she's a beauty, all right," Granda said. "Yes, a fine young thing and no mistake!"

Christy approached carefully. The filly accepted his hand stroking her neck.

"He's got a way with her," Christy heard the owner say. "She's usually nervous with strangers."

"How much?" Christy asked the dealer.

"I'd do a wee fella like you a good deal," he laughed.

Taking Christy's arm, Granda said firmly, "Come on now, Christy. Let's be away."

"I have the money, Granda, I'm not going home without her."

Granda sighed, "I know you've set your heart on her but what about your ma – she'd fry us for supper if we came home with a pony."

With Granda and his friends settled in the pub, Christy put a plan into action.

He made his way back to the filly and found the owner packing up to go.

"My granda went to arrange transport for the horse so he sent me to pay," said Christy breathlessly.

The man looked at him. "Well son, you're a bit young, but seeing as I need to be away and you've got cash, she's all yours!"

"What do you mean, you've bought her, Christy?" Granda looked
at him in astonishment.

"Just that," said Christy, holding on to the halter rope. "I'm
calling her Jasmine and the man's gone already so we'd better find a
horsebox to take us all home."

Granda kept rubbing his head and muttering as they rode home
in the cab of a horsebox. But Christy thought he was going to burst
with excitement. He'd done it! He had bought his very own pony.

Word soon got round.

"Christy's bought a horse . . . Christy's done it . . . Christy's got a grand filly!"

His friends crowded round while Christy prepared a space for Jasmine in the stables and food for the night.

Christy hoped Granda would tell his ma and da about Jasmine but Granda wasn't so sure. "Best say nothing till morning. I need to get up the courage." He laughed, but he looked nervous.

Christy wasn't going to tell without Granda there so he didn't say anything. Not even when Granda didn't appear the next day, or the one after. He went to school as usual and spent every spare moment with Jasmine. Now he could take his friends riding double. They galloped along the grass verges and raced across the playing fields.

Horsey was impressed.

"You've got a good one there, Christy. Has your ma seen her?"

"Me and Granda are going to tell her about Jasmine together," said Christy. "We'll probably do it today."

But he wasn't so sure, and it was troubling him that Ma didn't know.

"Your ma knows, Christy! She's heard!"
Declan came racing across the playing
fields. "She says you're to get rid of the
horse or she'll do it herself. What are you
going to do?"

Christy looked scared but he wasn't about to give up his horse. Not now.

"I'll run away with Jasmine and we'll live in the mountains," he said.
"I'd rather die than lose her now. And I'll tell Ma so myself!"

"I'm coming too," said Horsey.

"And me," said Declan.

They had quite a following by the time they reached Christy's flat.

"What's this, the cavalry?" said Ma. "Am I that scary, Christy?"
"I'll never give her up, Ma," said Christy. "You can't make me."
"This is my doing . . ." It was Granda, at last. "I'm sorry, lad, I should have told her."
"I might have known you'd be mixed up in this," Ma said crossly.

Horsey spoke next. "Mrs McCourt, there isn't a boy on the estate more able to look after a horse than your Christy."

"Listen to the man," said Da. "He's a sensible fella."

There was silence.

Ma looked at Da in surprise. Then she looked at Christy. Then she smiled. "Well then, I'd better take a closer look at this new member of the family."

"Well she looks like a winner to me!" said Ma, smiling at Christy.
Christy gave his ma a big hug, then his da and his grandad.
"Ma, when I'm a famous jockey, you'll get a new washing machine
and anything else you want."

"Enough of that chat," said Ma. "Away with you and your horse and let me get on with the dinner. There's a house full of young ones need feeding."

"And I've a hungry horse," said Christy. And off he rode.

The story of *Christy's Dream* is set in a real area of Dublin, where children look after their horses amidst the tower block estates. Meeting and photographing the boys of Ballymun, Caroline Binch was especially inspired because of her own love of horses:

"When I was at college, all I wanted was to be with horses. I loved the freedom and wildness that they represented."

Caroline Binch's meticulous watercolour paintings perfectly capture the details of the people and place and create an amazingly realistic image of this unique part of Ireland.

Christy's Dream is published as part of Mammoth's series of books with Irish authors, connections or settings. Other titles in this range include:

My Puffer Train	Mary Murphy	0 7497 3651 8
Some Things Change	Mary Murphy	0 7497 4212 7
Peg	Maddie Stewart	0 7497 3260 1
The Base	Carlo Gébler	0 7497 3133 8
Fierce Milly	Marilyn McLaughlin	0 7497 3731 X